BATMAN v SUPERMAN

DAWN OF JUSTICE

GUIDE TO THE CAPED CRUSADER

By Liz Marsham
Inspired by the film *Batman v Superman: Dawn of Justice*
written by Chris Terrio and David S. Goyer
Batman created by Bob Kane with Bill Finger

SCHOLASTIC INC.

ISBN 978-0-545-91627-1

10 9 8 7 6 5 4 3 2 1 16 17 18 19 20
Printed in the U.S.A. 40
First printing 2016
Book design by Cheung Tai

CONTENTS

Batman, Gotham City's Dark Knight

For twenty years, a masked man has been fighting crime in Gotham City. With his incredible gadgets and mastery of hand-to-hand combat, he helps keep the streets safe. But who is this strange vigilante known as Batman? Here you will learn all about him: his secret identity, his closest ally, the gadgets and vehicles that help him fight crime, and a mysterious new threat he must face!

GCPD

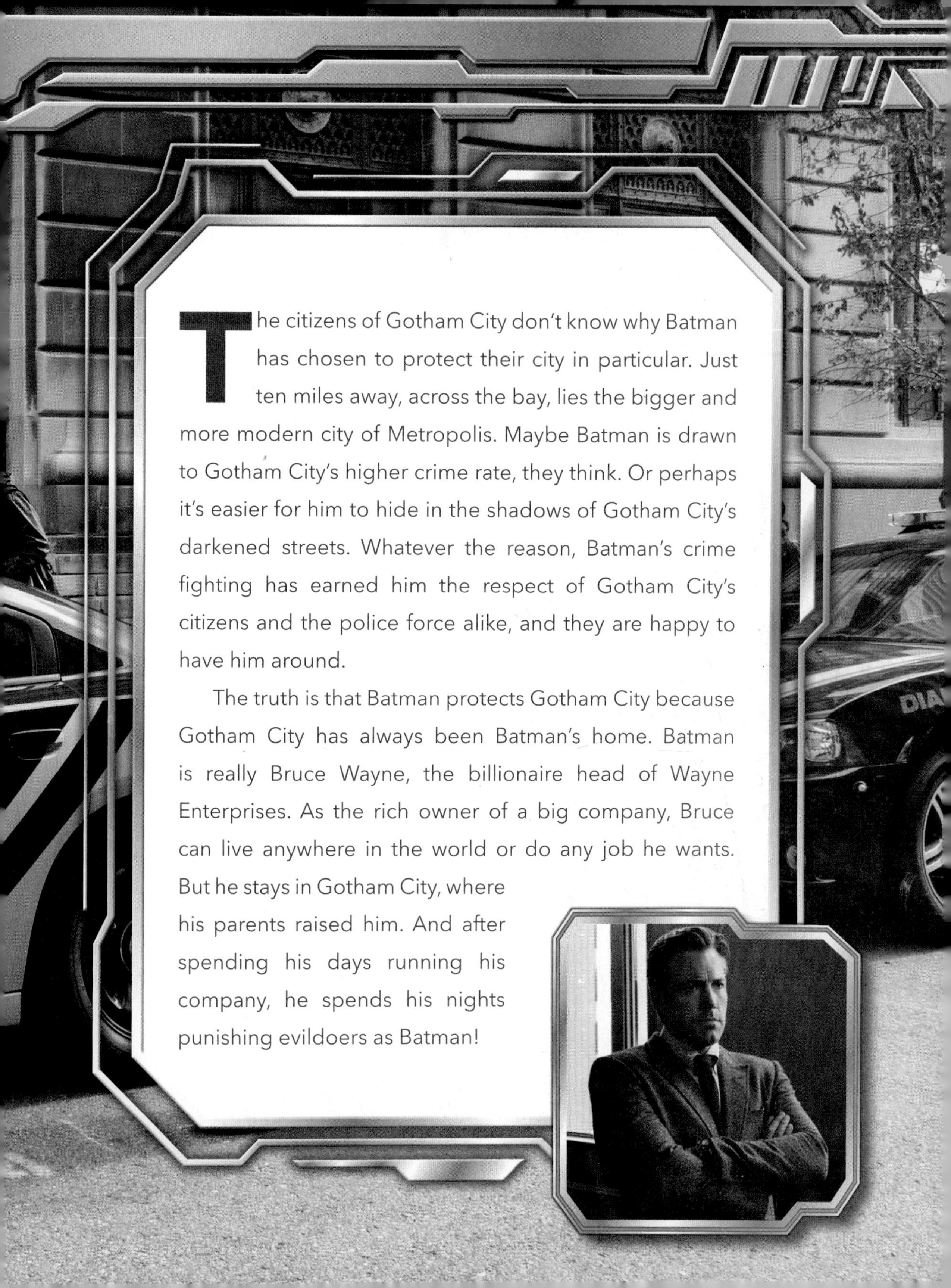

The citizens of Gotham City don't know why Batman has chosen to protect their city in particular. Just ten miles away, across the bay, lies the bigger and more modern city of Metropolis. Maybe Batman is drawn to Gotham City's higher crime rate, they think. Or perhaps it's easier for him to hide in the shadows of Gotham City's darkened streets. Whatever the reason, Batman's crime fighting has earned him the respect of Gotham City's citizens and the police force alike, and they are happy to have him around.

The truth is that Batman protects Gotham City because Gotham City has always been Batman's home. Batman is really Bruce Wayne, the billionaire head of Wayne Enterprises. As the rich owner of a big company, Bruce can live anywhere in the world or do any job he wants. But he stays in Gotham City, where his parents raised him. And after spending his days running his company, he spends his nights punishing evildoers as Batman!

BATMAN IS BORN

What drove Bruce Wayne to become Batman? The story begins one night when he was a boy. His parents, Thomas and Martha Wayne, took him to see a movie. Afterward, as they walked down the street, a criminal appeared and demanded their money. Then the robber got spooked and fired his gun, killing both of Bruce's parents in front of him. The robber was never caught, and the Waynes' murder remained one of Gotham City's greatest unsolved mysteries.

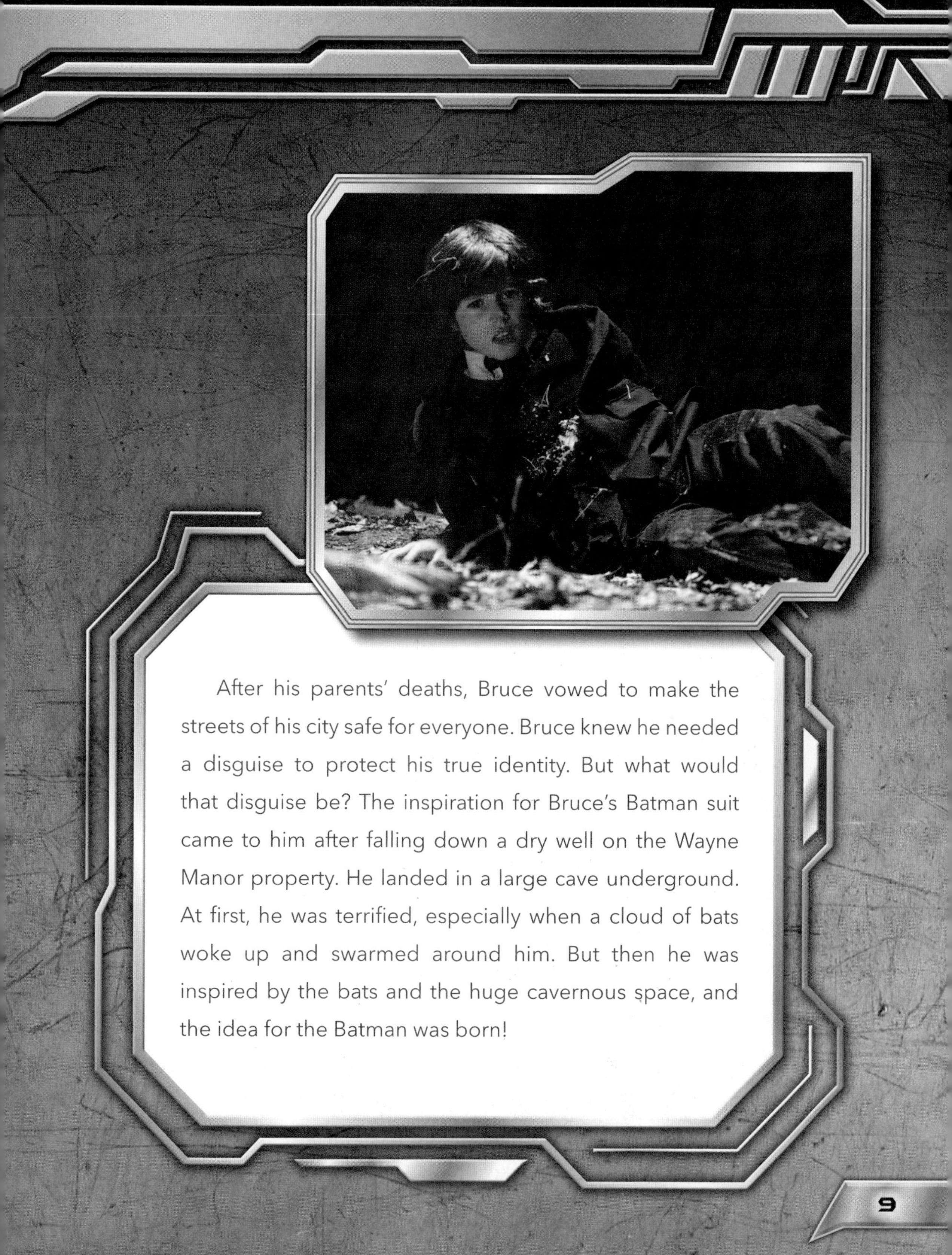

After his parents' deaths, Bruce vowed to make the streets of his city safe for everyone. Bruce knew he needed a disguise to protect his true identity. But what would that disguise be? The inspiration for Bruce's Batman suit came to him after falling down a dry well on the Wayne Manor property. He landed in a large cave underground. At first, he was terrified, especially when a cloud of bats woke up and swarmed around him. But then he was inspired by the bats and the huge cavernous space, and the idea for the Batman was born!

WAYNE MANOR

Bruce was raised in Wayne Manor, located on a large private estate on the edge of Gotham City. The manor had been the family's home for over a hundred years. Back when the Waynes first came to America, they were hunters and traders. Because of this they designed their family crest to show weapons and animals. Later, the Wayne fortune grew as they expanded their business into real estate, railroads, and oil.

Today, the manor is abandoned. Bruce left it so he could lead a simpler life, which gives him more time to focus on being Batman. But he visits sometimes to remember his parents and renew his dedication to keeping Gotham City safe.

The Wayne family crest.

ALFRED PENNYWORTH

The Waynes used to have a large personal staff to take care of their manor. But after his parents died, Bruce decided he didn't need servants. Now, only one person remains: Alfred Pennyworth. Alfred started out working for the Wayne family as a bodyguard, then became Bruce's legal guardian and confidant when Thomas and Martha died. Alfred has also chosen to leave the decaying manor, living in a comfortable trailer on the Wayne Estate. Publically, Alfred is known as Bruce Wayne's chief of security.

But what the public doesn't know is that Alfred is also an invaluable help to Batman. He is a former officer in the SAS, the Special Air Service unit of the British Army. In the SAS, he received training in several areas, such as weapons, intelligence gathering, medicine, and piloting all sorts of vehicles and aircraft. Today he puts all of that training to good use helping Batman stay protected and well equipped in his fight against crime.

Alfred adds an upgrade to Batman's armor.

MANOR NO MORE

Today, Bruce lives close to the old manor, on the shore of the nearby lake. Surrounded on three sides by trees and the fourth by open water, his new house is made out of large glass panes held in place by dark metal. Batman may have to hide in the shadows, but when Bruce is at home, he can feel like he's out in the open.

THE BATCAVE

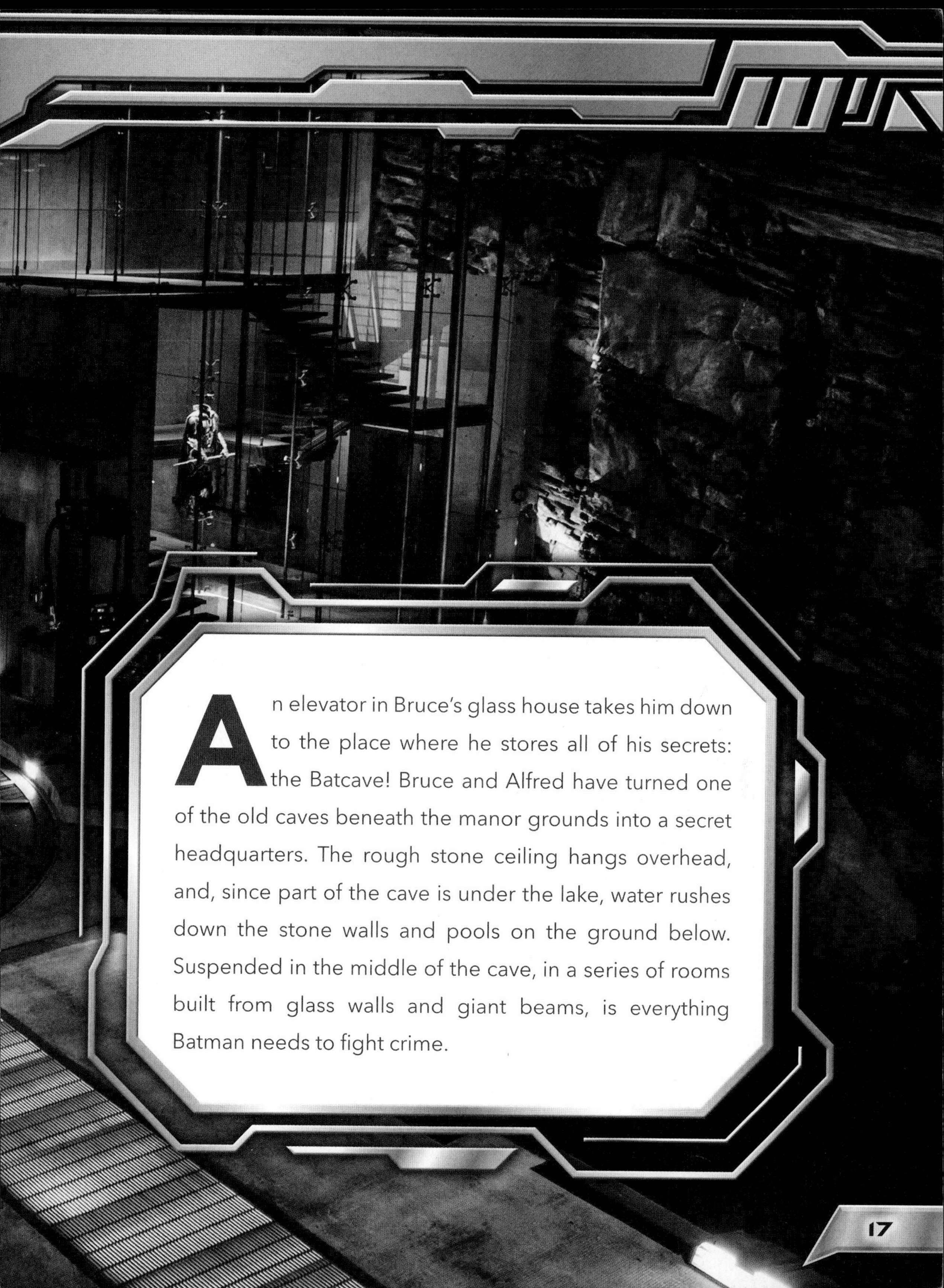

An elevator in Bruce's glass house takes him down to the place where he stores all of his secrets: the Batcave! Bruce and Alfred have turned one of the old caves beneath the manor grounds into a secret headquarters. The rough stone ceiling hangs overhead, and, since part of the cave is under the lake, water rushes down the stone walls and pools on the ground below. Suspended in the middle of the cave, in a series of rooms built from glass walls and giant beams, is everything Batman needs to fight crime.

INSIDE THE BATCAVE

There are several sections to the Batcave: workbenches for building and repairing equipment, lab benches for doing experiments, an armory to store weapons and armor, and a garage to store and repair all of Batman's vehicles. And, of course, there is the massive computer that serves as Batman's information hub.

To keep Batman's identity a secret, Bruce and Alfred had to build everything in the Batcave by themselves. With Bruce's fortune, they have easy access to the most high-tech tools and materials, but some things had to be learned by trial and error. By now they've had many years to figure out what works and what doesn't, so many items in the cave show signs of having been repaired and improved over time.

The Batcave has its own laboratory for analyzing evidence.

THE BATCAVE COMPUTER

This giant computer console is Batman's main source of information. In addition to being a powerful computer, it has live hookups to police radio feeds and all major news sources. Like everything else in the Batcave, the computer was built over time, and so several different stages of technology are being used at once. For instance, the console is hooked up to both classic computer keyboards and more modern touchscreens.

07A
CASE FILE 0714 2015 07A

THE BATCAVE'S GARAGE

On the lowest level of the Batcave is the garage. A driveway leads to a secret exit for ground vehicles like the Batmobile. A landing pad is set up beneath a large opening in the Batcave's ceiling, so Batman's aerial vehicles like the Batwing can take off and land. And a special computer console allows Bruce and Alfred to examine the Batcave vehicles, so they can be easily fixed and upgraded.

Alfred expertly repairs the Batcave's many vehicles.

THE BATMOBILE

The vehicle Batman uses most often is the Batmobile. The most obvious thing about it is how big it is: twenty-two feet long and eleven feet wide in the back! Its size means criminals are more likely to be afraid of it, and Batman also needs all that room to fit in the amazing features he uses to fight crime.

Most importantly, the entire car is thickly armored to keep Batman safe. Even the tires are bulletproof and fireproof. All that armor could make the Batmobile clunky to drive, so hydraulics have been installed along the sides for additional flexibility. When the hydraulics are pulled in, the car hunches up in the middle, which allows for better handling and aiming of its various weapons and gadgets. Then, when speed and a low profile are the most important things, the hydraulics lengthen, and the Batmobile stretches out and gets low and sleek.

ON THE STREETS

The last thing criminals want to see is the Batmobile headed straight for them! From the front, the bulletproof windshield and the various weapons on the hood are clearly visible. From non-lethal bullets to tracking devices, the Batmobile has it all. There is also a bank of countermeasures beneath the hood. For example, one sends out a shimmery type of smoke that confuses enemy weapons like rockets and missiles, making them explode before they hit the car.

THE COCKPIT OF THE BATMOBILE

Inside the Batmobile is an array of buttons, switches, panels, and diagnostic devices. There are so many extra controls and screens, Bruce and Alfred had to install a special, small steering wheel that doesn't take up as much room! Everything in the Batmobile is designed to be high-tech, while serving a very specific purpose.

The main thermal-imaging screen uses the heat of surrounding objects to show Batman everything in front of and around the car. This way he can drive through the darkest alleys or the deepest fog safely. He can even leave his headlights off if he wants to take the bad guys by surprise.

AERIAL SCAN
ANTI POLICE
DANGER

BATMOBILE GADGETS

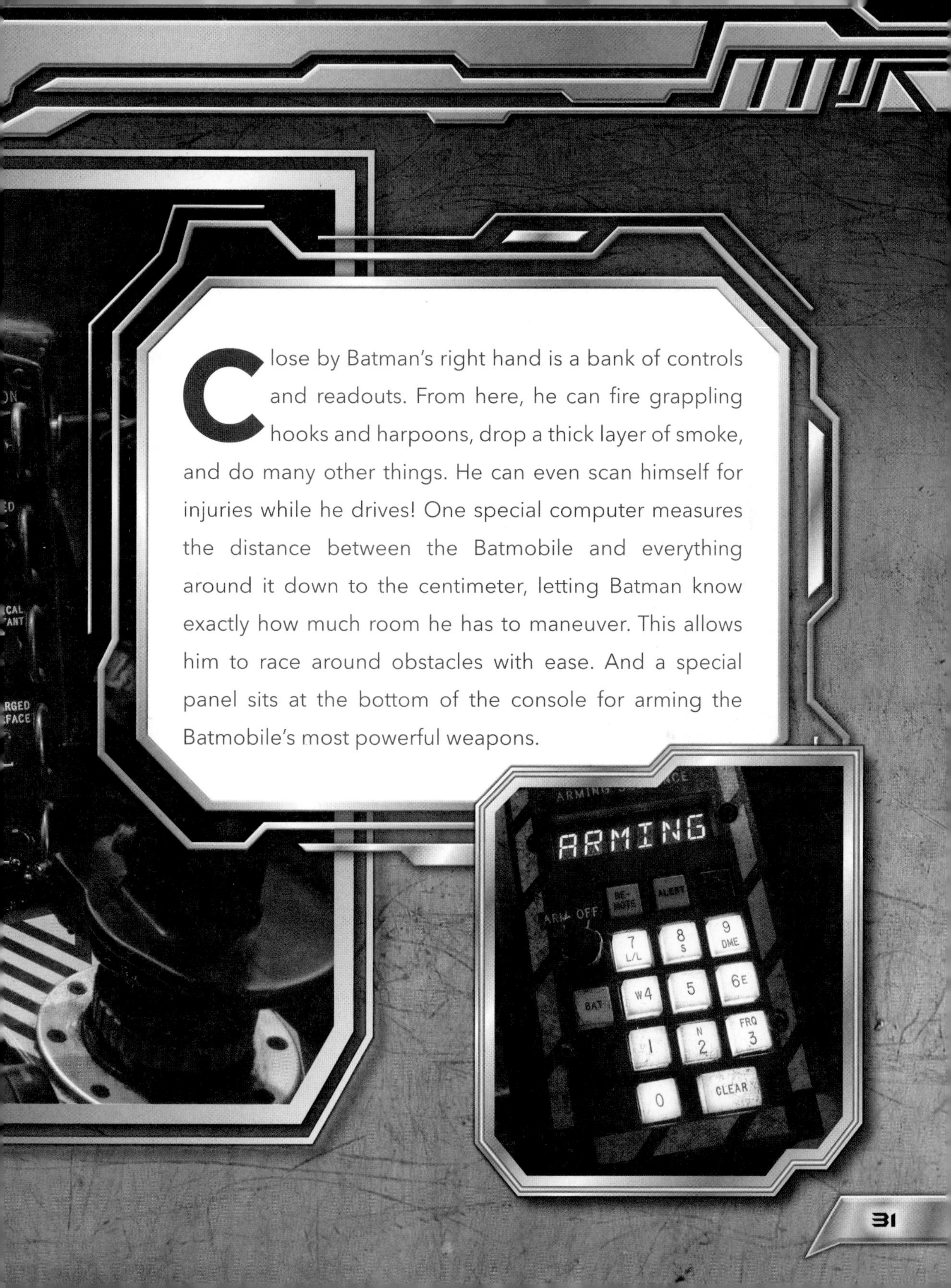

Close by Batman's right hand is a bank of controls and readouts. From here, he can fire grappling hooks and harpoons, drop a thick layer of smoke, and do many other things. He can even scan himself for injuries while he drives! One special computer measures the distance between the Batmobile and everything around it down to the centimeter, letting Batman know exactly how much room he has to maneuver. This allows him to race around obstacles with ease. And a special panel sits at the bottom of the console for arming the Batmobile's most powerful weapons.

THE BATWING

Sometimes Batman needs to take to the sky to fight crime. So Bruce and Alfred have created a modern jet called the Batwing! The Batwing can take off and land without any runway at all. It travels straight up and down by folding its wings over the cockpit and rotating its jets to point at the ground. These special jets allow the Batwing to get into the Batcave or land in any other tight space.

When it's time to race through the air, the wings fold flat and the jets move into their horizontal position. The Batwing's powerful engines engage, and the plane roars to the rescue at incredible speeds.

And the Batwing has a secret: it can be flown remotely, without anyone inside the cockpit at all! The computer in the Batcave can transform into another cockpit, allowing Batman to use all the features of the Batwing without actually being on the scene.

THE ARMORY IN THE BATCAVE

Batman has armor and gadgets for any occasion, but he needs a place to keep them. The armory section of the Batcave has everything he needs: weapons racks and cases for storage, and workbenches and rigs for building and repair.

When Bruce and Alfred are building a suit, they use a high-tech rig to test the pieces as they are completed. This lets them see how everything is coming together even before the suit is finished.

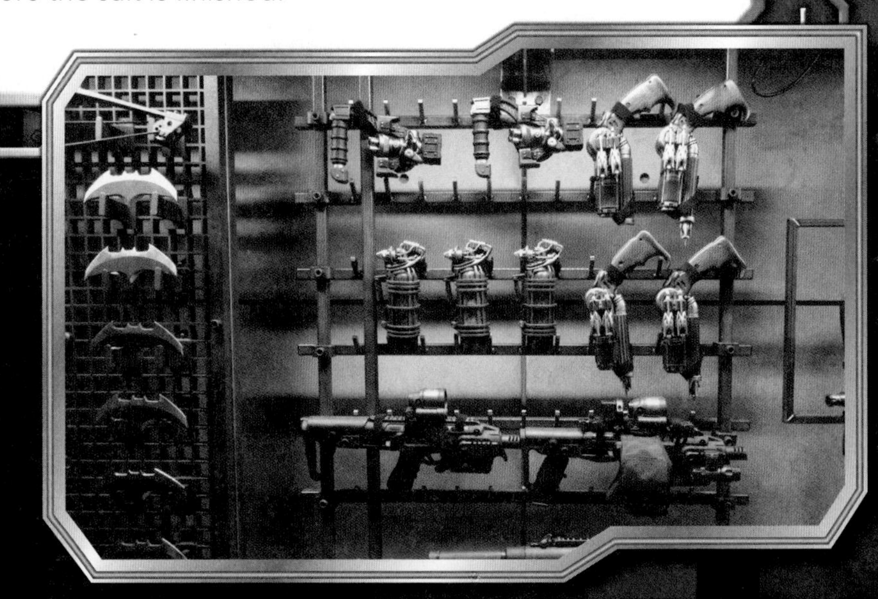

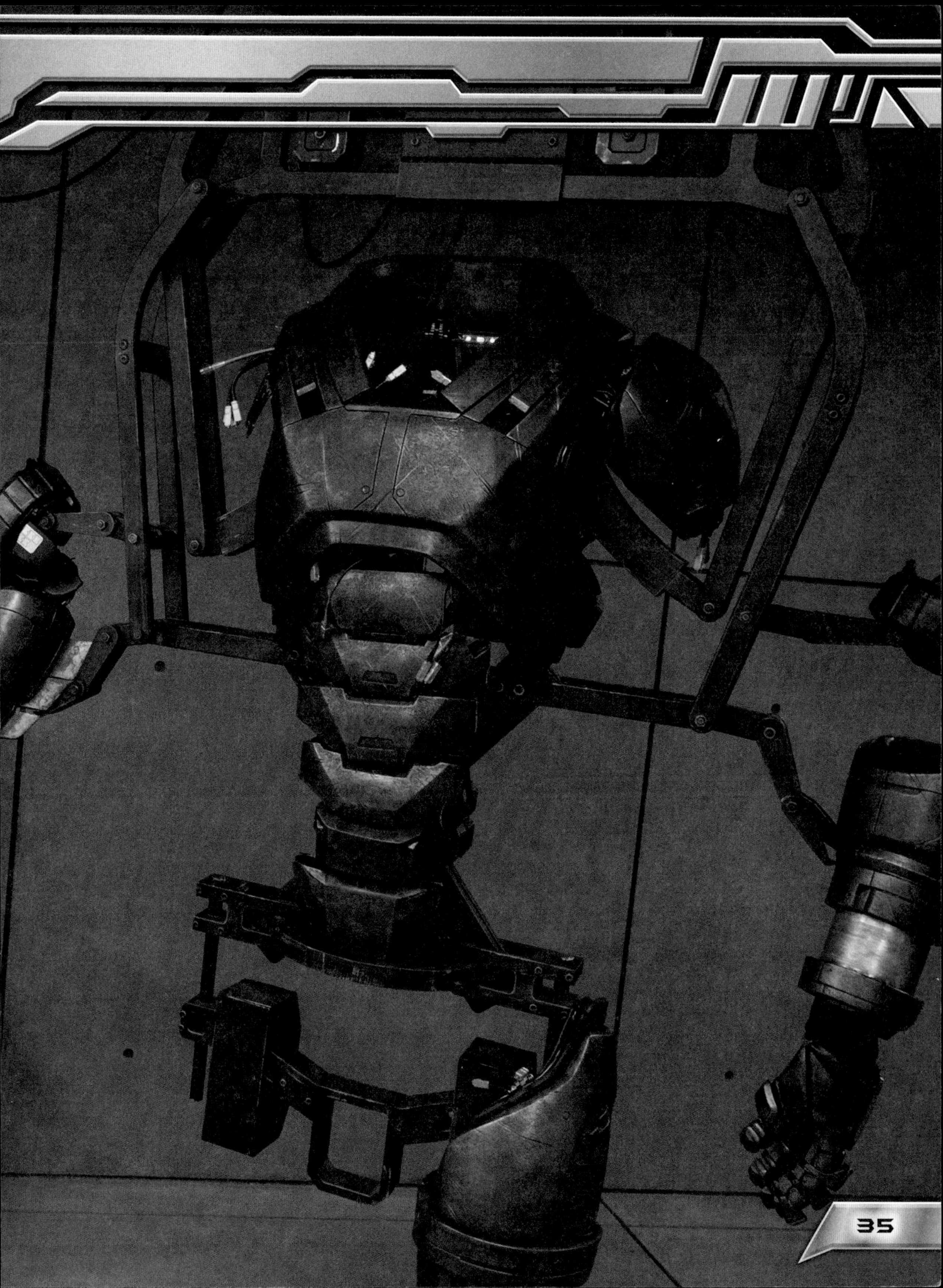

THE BATSUIT CASE

When he and Alfred aren't repairing or improving it, Bruce Wayne keeps his main Batsuit in a special, secure case in the Batcave. The case opens with a handprint scanner, so only Bruce can access it. He presses his hand to the scanner, watches the glass case rotate, and hears the door whoosh back. Inside is the suit that will protect him during another night of fighting crime.

THE BATSUIT

Bruce and Alfred had to make some difficult choices when they first designed the Batsuit. Body armor is very safe, but it's also heavy and bulky, so it could slow Batman down. On the other hand, lighter fabrics allow Batman to be faster and more agile, but those fabrics don't protect him as well against knives or bullets. As the years went by and they continued to tweak the design of the suit, they incorporated more lightweight, high-tech materials.

Today's Batsuit is reinforced with the latest in bulletproof fabrics and lightweight plates, as well as a fireproof cape, giving Batman the best of both worlds.

THE COWL

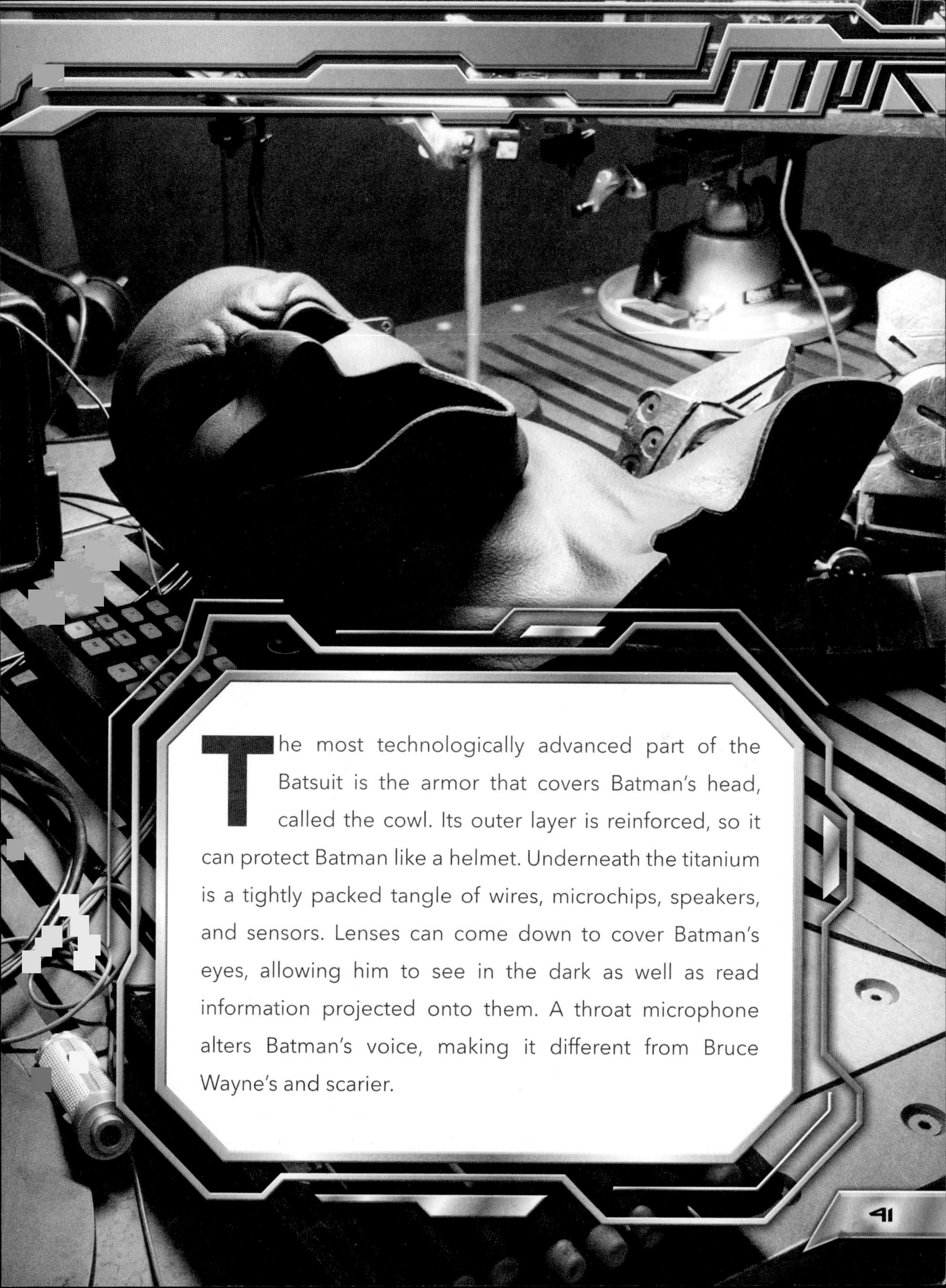

The most technologically advanced part of the Batsuit is the armor that covers Batman's head, called the cowl. Its outer layer is reinforced, so it can protect Batman like a helmet. Underneath the titanium is a tightly packed tangle of wires, microchips, speakers, and sensors. Lenses can come down to cover Batman's eyes, allowing him to see in the dark as well as read information projected onto them. A throat microphone alters Batman's voice, making it different from Bruce Wayne's and scarier.

BATMAN'S WEAPONS

Batman's first priority is stopping criminals without killing them. So he and Alfred have created several types of very special weapons, and Batman knows exactly how to use each one to its best effect. He can knock a gun out of a criminal's hand with a Batarang, trip another enemy with a grappling line, and stop a third bad guy with a sleeping dart—all using the weapons from his personal armory.

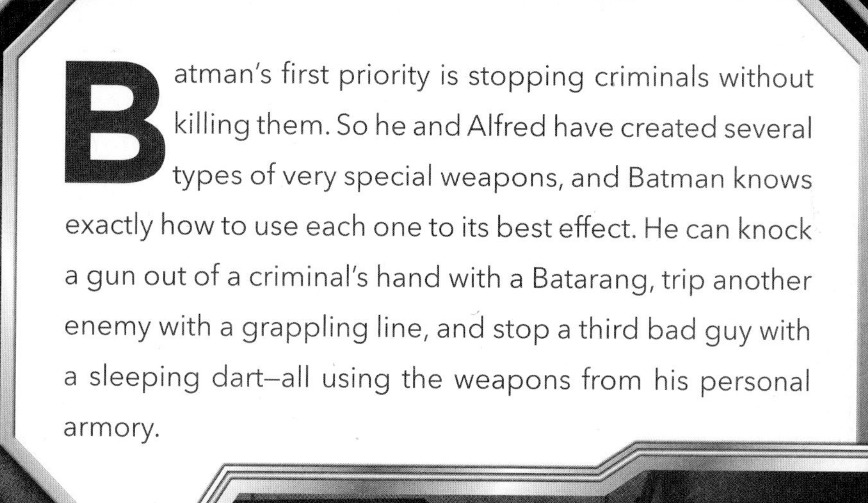

BATARANGS

Batman's most recognizable weapons are his Batarangs. Batman can throw the Batarangs with pinpoint accuracy, making them valuable in a lot of different situations. A well thrown Batarang can knock away a weapon, hit a button, cut a wire, break a window . . . and those are just a few of the things Batman has used them for!

Batman also leaves Batarangs behind when he has been at a crime scene. This teaches other criminals to fear him, and it lets the police know that he has been there to help.

The Batarang is Batman's calling card.

GRAPNEL GUN

Another of Batman's most used gadgets is his grapnel gun. Like everything else in the Batcave, the grapnel guns are handmade by Bruce and Alfred. But because there hasn't been a need to upgrade these guns with new technology, their homemade nature shows through in their wooden handles and rough edges.

Like the Batarangs, Batman can use the grapnel gun in many different ways. He can fire it up the side of a building to pull himself onto a ledge, or he can fire it between buildings to travel quickly along Gotham City's skyline. In closer quarters, he can fire it across a room and let it pull him from one side to the other, confusing enemies. And he can use it to create traps, firing a strong cable for his opponents to trip over or run into.

NEW GADGETS

No complete list of Batman's gadgets exists, because he and Alfred are always inventing new ones. After every battle, Batman thinks of new ways that he can safely and securely catch criminals. From smoke grenades to whatever Batman needs, there's no doubt that Bruce and Alfred can build it in the Batcave!

These smoke grenades help Batman take down villains and disappear from sight!

BAT-SIGNAL

Batman finds and catches a lot of criminals on his own. But when Gotham City needs him in a hurry, they can always turn on the Bat-Signal. The Bat-Signal is a huge searchlight that projects a bat-shaped emblem onto the night sky, so that Batman can see it and rush to respond.

But soon the Bat-Signal will be used for a new purpose . . .

THE CLASH WITH SUPERMAN

Batman has been worried about Superman's growing power for years. Bruce Wayne was in Metropolis when a ship full of Kryptonian invaders began destroying the city. Even though Superman eventually saved the day, Bruce saw how much was lost during the fight. The fact that Superman refuses to answer to any government only increases Bruce's fears. Bruce is keeping a close watch on Superman, learning as much as he can about this alien "hero."

Bruce runs to help during the Battle of Metropolis.

ARMORED BATSUIT

Confronting Superman could be dangerous business, but Batman always comes prepared. Bruce has a special armored Batsuit that could protect him if he ever needed to defend Gotham City from an alien foe. The armor is the strongest available, and lined with lead, making the suit incredibly heavy. But it carries an internal power source, so Batman can move easily in it. The lenses over Batman's eyes help Bruce analyze his enemy's movements and look for weaknesses.

What Comes Next for Gotham City's Dark Knight?

Bruce Wayne has been fighting crime as Batman for twenty years now. He has honed his body, his skills, his intellect, and his equipment over all that time, and he is a match for any criminal on Earth. But Batman has never met anyone like Superman before!

BATMAN v SUPERMAN™

DAWN OF JUSTICE

GUIDE TO THE MAN OF STEEL

By Liz Marsham

Inspired by the film *Batman v Superman: Dawn of Justice*
written by Chris Terrio and David S. Goyer
Superman created by Jerry Siegel and Joe Shuster
By special arrangement with the Jerry Siegel family

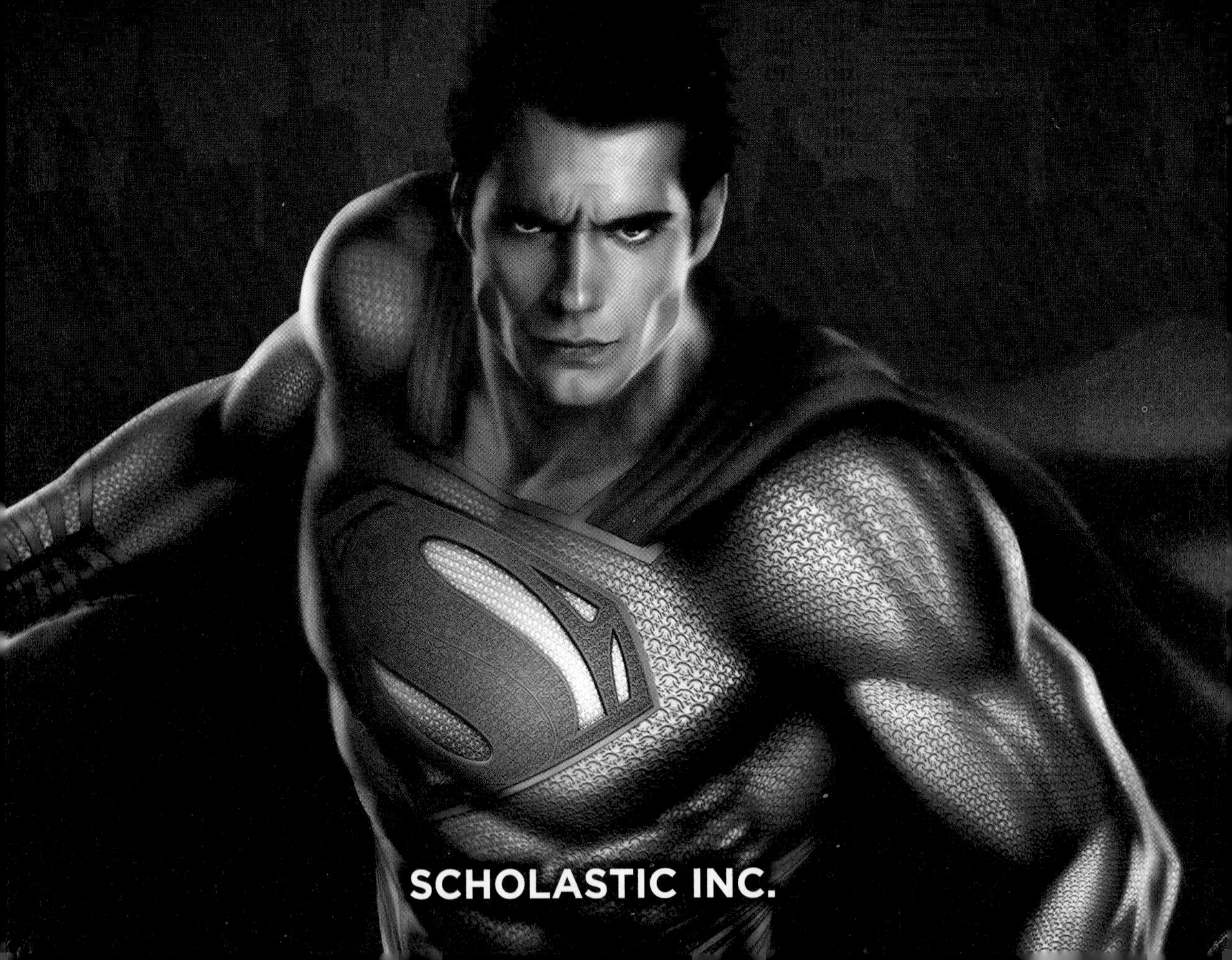

SCHOLASTIC INC.

ISBN 978-0-545-91627-1

10 9 8 7 6 5 4 3 2 1 16 17 18 19 20
Printed in the U.S.A. 40
First printing 2016
Book design by Cheung Tai

CONTENTS

SUPERMAN, A SUPER HERO FOR EVERYONE

For over thirty years, Superman lived in secret. He hid his amazing abilities until one day when he bravely saved the Earth from an alien invasion. Since then, many has come to know him as a Super Hero from another planet who uses his incredible powers to defend humanity. But this mysterious alien has plenty of secrets to discover. Here you will learn where Superman came from, what he can do, and what the future has in store for the Man of Steel!

THE PLANET KRYPTON

Millions of miles from Earth, a small planet once orbited a red sun. This planet, named Krypton, was home to an ancient civilization of people who looked exactly like humans. Over a hundred thousand years, the Kryptonians used up all of the planet's resources. They strip-mined the surface of their homeworld until it was almost barren, and then most of them moved into caves under the ground.

There were only a few places left where wildlife, like the huge Rondor beasts, could still roam free. And only a few Kryptonians still lived above the surface—like Jor-El, Krypton's most brilliant scientist, and his wife, Lara. The couple lived in an observatory on top of a cliff, overlooking the ruins of their once-beautiful planet.

Rondor beasts have six legs and spiky shells.

THE HOUSE OF EL

The Kryptonians were incredibly advanced, but their technology used large amounts of power. When all other sources of energy ran out, they began mining the molten core of their homeworld.

Jor-El tried to warn the leaders of Krypton that mining the core would ruin the planet and cause it to collapse. But they didn't listen to him. The Council refused to evacuate the planet.

So, Jor-El and Lara made a plan that would allow one Kryptonian to survive: their newborn son, Kal-El. They knew they had to send their baby to safety even if they couldn't save themselves. They searched the universe to find a special planet: Earth, where Kal would look just like any other child. They built him a rocket with everything he would need to survive the journey. Finally, they included a command key that would one day teach Kal all about them and about Krypton. With hardly any time to spare before the planet collapsed, Jor-El and Lara launched the rocket and sent Kal speeding toward his new home.

The command key was shaped like the House of El's family crest.

SMALLVILLE, SUPERMAN'S NEW HOME

After a long journey through space, Kal-El's rocket crash-landed in Smallville, Kansas. Smallville is, as the name suggests, a little town. Full of wide-open fields and farms, and far from major cities, Smallville was the perfect place for Kal to grow up. Its sleepiness and seclusion meant that a little boy could learn to use his big abilities without drawing unwanted attention.

THE KENTS

Just as Smallville was the perfect place for Kal to grow up, Jonathan and Martha Kent were the perfect people to raise him. When the Kents came upon the crashed rocket and found a baby inside, they knew right away that the boy was an alien. Without knowing anything else about where he came from, they decided to raise him as their own. This generosity and openheartedness was one of the many wonderful examples they set for their new son, whom they named Clark.

CLARK DISCOVERS HIS SUPERPOWERS

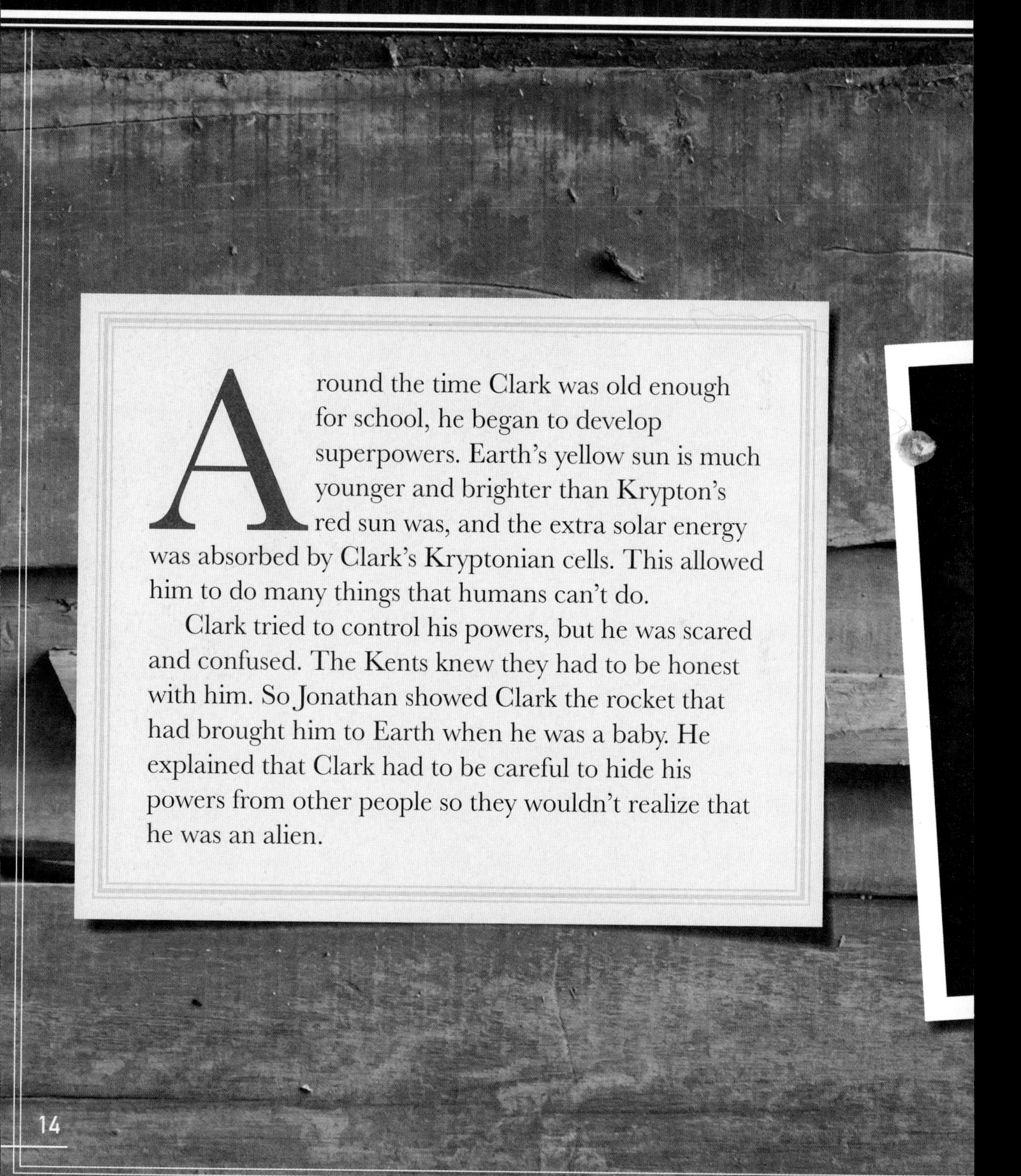

Around the time Clark was old enough for school, he began to develop superpowers. Earth's yellow sun is much younger and brighter than Krypton's red sun was, and the extra solar energy was absorbed by Clark's Kryptonian cells. This allowed him to do many things that humans can't do.

Clark tried to control his powers, but he was scared and confused. The Kents knew they had to be honest with him. So Jonathan showed Clark the rocket that had brought him to Earth when he was a baby. He explained that Clark had to be careful to hide his powers from other people so they wouldn't realize that he was an alien.

SUPER-HEARING

Hiding his abilities was difficult for Clark at first. One of the hardest powers to control was his super-hearing. At school, he couldn't concentrate on what his teacher was saying when he could also hear her heart beating, a phone ringing down the hall, the birds chirping outside . . . not to mention every word everyone else in the building was saying!

Clark learned to control his super-hearing by focusing on one thing at a time.

Now Superman can use his hearing with amazing sensitivity. He is no longer bothered by loud or overlapping noises, and he is able to pick out a single voice from miles away or attend to the softest sound in the middle of a screaming crowd.

X-RAY VISION

Another power that Clark had a hard time controlling was his X-ray vision. It was great to be able to see through walls when he wanted to, but it was awful to be talking to people and suddenly see their skeletons through their skin! Martha helped Clark accept his strange power and kept him from being overwhelmed by the new images.

After years of practice, Clark has honed his vision to pinpoint accuracy. He can see clearly through a building, or he can tell people standing next to him exactly what's in their pockets. Between his X-ray vision and his super-hearing, villains can't keep secrets from Superman!

SUPER-STRENGTH

With his cells full of our sun's radiation, Superman becomes incredibly strong. Clark first used his super-strength as a teenager to save a bus full of his classmates. It was risky to reveal his strength to so many people, but Clark knew it was the right thing to do.

As he grew older, Clark also grew stronger. As Superman, he can lift trucks and hurl them away as if they were baseballs. He can bend steel bars or crush diamonds in his bare hands. He can hold thousands of tons of weight over his head. And he can do it all again and again without even getting tired.

In high school, Clark used his strength to stop a bus from sinking.

INVULNERABILITY

Because his cells are so strong, it's nearly impossible for Superman to get hurt. He can stand in a fiery inferno or walk across the freezing ridges of Antarctica and be perfectly comfortable. Bullets and blades bounce right off of his super-strong skin. He can withstand the force of an explosion. It seems like nothing on Earth can stop Superman!

When Clark was a boy, he tried very hard not to use his powers. But once he grew up and found a safe place to test himself, he wanted to see what would happen if he gathered his strength and leapt into the air. To his surprise and delight, Clark discovered that he could fly!

At first, he just hurled himself into the air and came crashing right back down to the ground. But quickly he learned to control his new power, and he is now able to fly for as long as he wants. He can even hover in midair or fly all the way to outer space and back!

SUPER-SPEED

The solar energy in Superman's cells also allows him to move faster than any human . . . even faster than any human can see! In an instant, he can accelerate until he's moving swifter than the speed of sound, leaving a thunderous sonic boom in his wake. His reflexes are equally quick, which is very important. With his lightning reflexes, he can think and react in time to control his actions when moving at super-speed—otherwise he wouldn't be able to avoid anything in his way. Superman wouldn't be nearly as heroic if he crashed into things every time he tried to race to the rescue!

HEAT VISION

One of Superman's more unusual powers is his heat vision. He can channel the energy in his cells into a beam of red light that shoots out of his eyes. He has total control over both the width and the strength of this energy beam, making it useful in many different situations. A gentle beam can heat up a doorknob. A stronger and tightly focused beam can cut through a sheet of metal like a laser. Or Superman can unleash a large and super-strong beam that acts as a blast of energy.

SUPERMAN'S KRYPTONIAN HERITAGE

Once Clark knew where he came from, he searched the world, hoping to find more evidence of the Kryptonians. Finally Clark discovered an ancient Kryptonian scout ship buried in a glacier in the Canadian Arctic. He put the key Jor-El and Lara had given him into a machine on the ship. To his surprise, a hologram of Jor-El appeared!

Jor-El taught Clark many things about Kryptonian history, and he gave him a very special gift: a suit bearing the symbol of the House of El. Wearing this symbol, which means "hope" in Kryptonian and also looks like the letter *S*, was the perfect way for Superman to represent the best of both his worlds. Now he was truly ready to be a hero!

SUPERMAN'S MISSION, SUPERMAN'S SECRET

Jonathan Kent was afraid that if people found out about Clark's powers, they'd reject him and maybe even try to hurt him. But Clark couldn't ignore the fact that people needed his help. So Clark came up with a compromise. Wearing a special suit and cape, he does his good deeds in disguise as Superman.

Many people around the world recognize Superman as a hero.

Now Superman helps people all around the world, saving them from earthquakes, fires, floods, and other danger. Everyone knows about Superman, and they know all the amazing things that Superman can do . . . but they don't know that Superman is also Clark Kent!

METROPOLIS TODAY

These days, Clark Kent no longer lives in sleepy Smallville. Instead, he makes his home in busy Metropolis—a major American city, home to millions of people as well as several big businesses like LexCorp. For years, Metropolis grew and thrived, in good times and bad. But recently, Metropolis experienced the worst tragedy in its history.

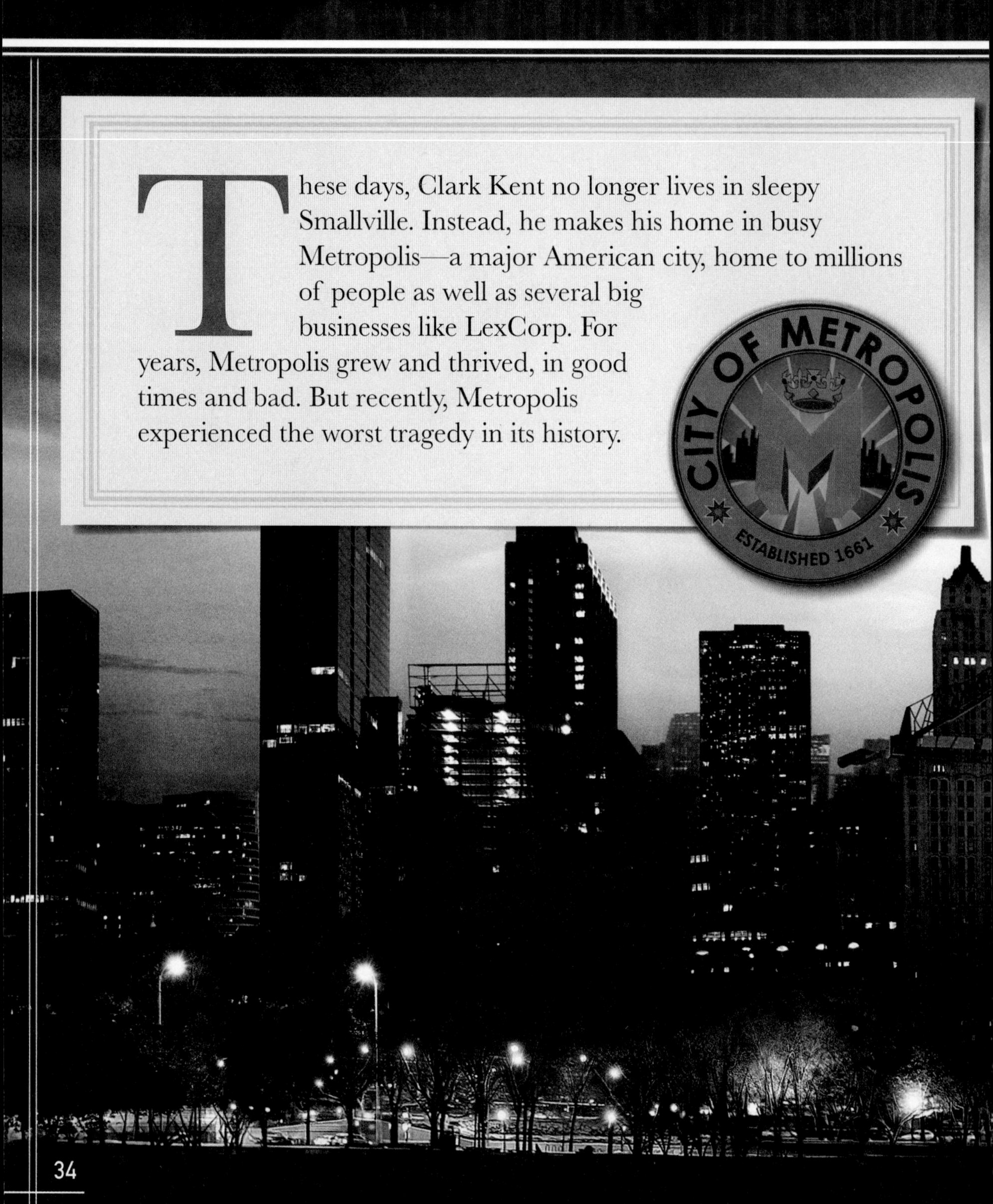

METROPOLIS IN PERIL

One day, a group of Kryptonian criminals arrived on Earth in their prison spaceship called the *Black Zero*. These criminals had escaped the destruction of their planet, and they wanted to take over Earth. They planned to make Earth into a new Kryptonian homeworld. They brought a World Engine: a powerful piece of Kryptonian technology that shoots a huge energy beam into planets, changing their structure and atmosphere.

The criminals flew the pieces of the World Engine into position, one over the Indian Ocean and one directly over Metropolis, and turned them on. The entire Earth was in danger, but the destruction was starting right in the center of Metropolis!

THE BATTLE OF METROPOLIS

Superman needed to break the piece of the World Engine over the Indian Ocean, which would shut it down and save the planet. But the World Engine shot out powerful arms to block Superman and keep him from getting too close. Finally, he was able to break through the arms and fly directly through the center of the craft, smashing it into bits.

Then he flew at super-speed back to Metropolis to take on the *Black Zero*. With the help of Lois Lane and some brave American soldiers, he was able to defeat the criminals and stop the Kryptonian invasion.

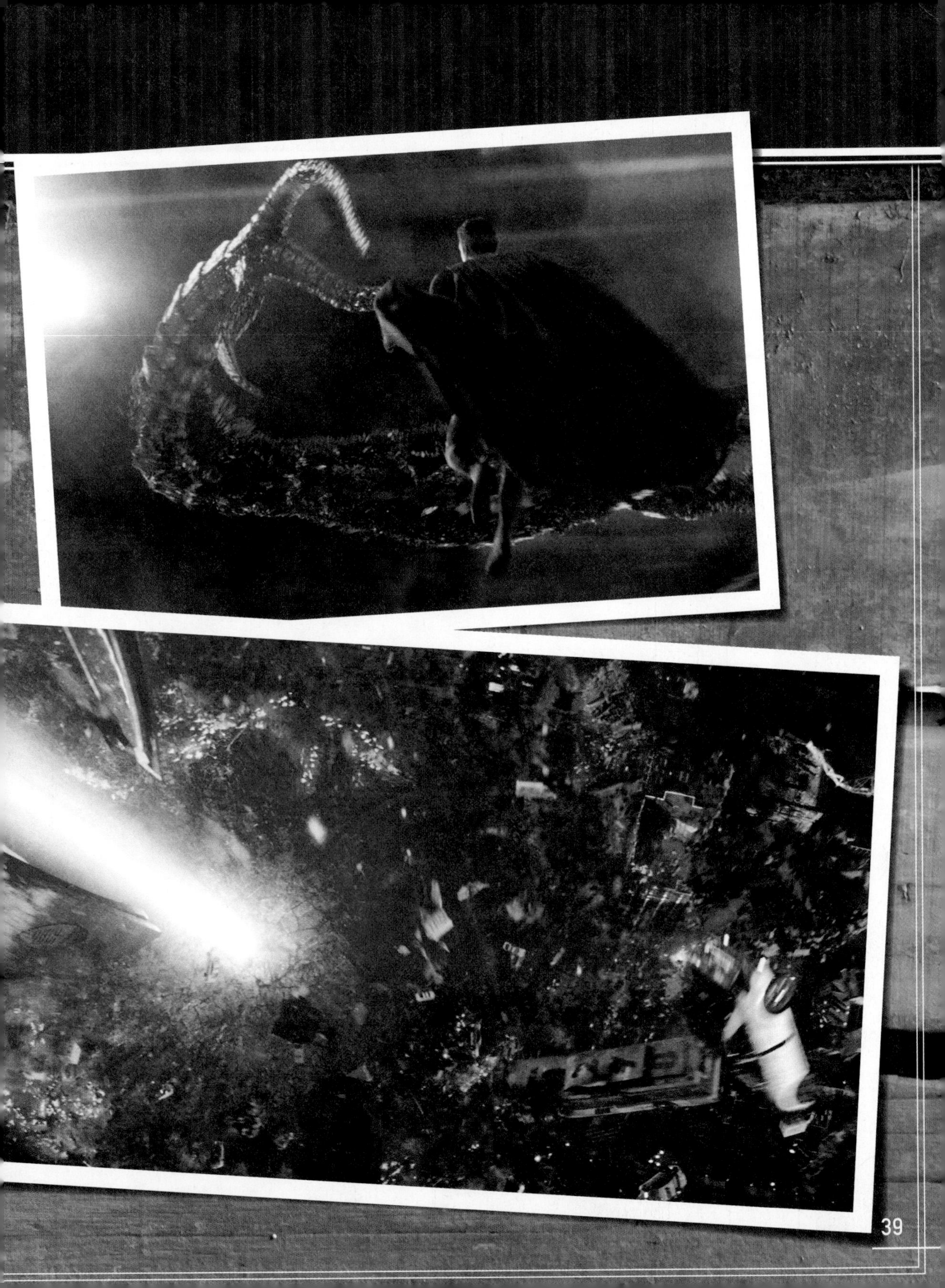

HONORING SUPERMAN

Two years later, the place where the *Black Zero* crashed into Metropolis was made into a memorial park. At one end of the park, a Superman statue was erected, in honor of his heroic acts that day. The statue has become a tourist attraction, as people come to pay their respects to Superman and remember how he saved the Earth from destruction.

SUPERMAN'S SKEPTICS

Even though many people around the world have embraced Superman as a hero, some are still wary of him. After all, everyone knows that the Kryptonian invaders came from the same planet as Superman. And everyone knows that Superman doesn't answer to anyone—no government or military power can control him. Even though Superman always uses his powers to help others, some people can't bring themselves to trust him. This mistrust means that he has to keep hiding his real identity while disguised as Clark Kent. But he's always ready to help people—even those who are suspicious of him—as Superman!

In order for Superman to help the most people, Clark decided to take a job that would give him access to all kinds of information. So he moved to Metropolis and became a reporter for the *Daily Planet*. As a reporter, Clark can investigate things without attracting attention, and then use his knowledge to figure out where Superman is needed the most.

LOIS LANE

Clark's girlfriend, Lois Lane, also works at the *Daily Planet*. She is a very successful investigative journalist. Her favorite stories are the hardest ones—when her pursuit of the truth takes her into dangerous places. She has interviewed terrorist leaders in war zones and soldiers on the battlefield. She has even pried secrets out of the most tight-lipped government officials.

So when she learned that Superman existed, it's no wonder that she quickly figured out his secret identity. But then, rather than exposing his secret, she helped him to hide the clues so that no one else could follow her trail. And now, if she needs help, she has Superman to back her up!

THE *DAILY PLANET*

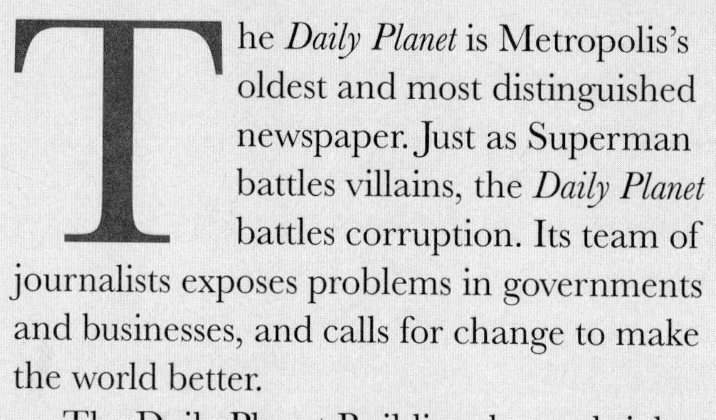

The *Daily Planet* is Metropolis's oldest and most distinguished newspaper. Just as Superman battles villains, the *Daily Planet* battles corruption. Its team of journalists exposes problems in governments and businesses, and calls for change to make the world better.

The Daily Planet Building, located right in the heart of Metropolis, is one of the city's landmarks. Visitors love posing with the large bronze planet in the lobby.

DAILY PLANET

ACE REPORTERS

Perry White is the editor in chief of the *Daily Planet*, which makes him Clark Kent and Lois Lane's boss. He places a lot of importance on integrity and excellent journalism, so he appreciates Lois's hard work and thorough investigating. But he also knows that newspapers have to be successful to survive, and hard-hitting stories don't always appeal to everyone. So he needs to strike a balance. Since Clark is a newer and less-experienced reporter, Perry sometimes assigns him lighter stories to attract more readers. Clark understands why Perry wants him to cover sports teams and store openings. But Clark must strike a careful balance of his own: on one hand the needs of the *Daily Planet*, and on the other hand his own need for information that he can use as Superman.

Perry assigns reporters different stories at their staff meeting.

LEX LUTHOR, GENIUS BILLIONAIRE

Clark is also very interested in a genius named Lex Luthor. Lex is the owner of LexCorp, a giant technology company headquartered in Metropolis. Under Lex's supervision, LexCorp is playing a big part in rebuilding those areas damaged by the Battle of Metropolis.

But Clark can tell that Lex's agenda goes beyond leading the computer industry or restoring Metropolis. Why, for instance, is a tech businessman so interested in Superman? Considering Lex's nearly unlimited budget and resources, he could be hiding some pretty big secrets.

LEXCORP HQ

LexCorp is Lex's hugely successful technology company. It was started in the 1960s by Lex's father. But Lex's father didn't see a future in computers, which held the company back. Only after young Lex inherited the company did it achieve its great success.

The current LexCorp headquarters in Metropolis was built in the 1980s. On the inside, though, the building has been remodeled to look sleek and modern.

XCORP

LEXCORP TOWER

LexCorp is now the most successful company in America, and it's growing faster than the current headquarters can contain. Lex has taken the opportunity to break ground on a gigantic new skyscraper called LexCorp Tower. The huge, modern structure isn't completed yet, but already it dominates the Metropolis skyline. The tower serves as a reminder of Lex's vision and his ego, both of which extend far beyond a few buildings.

INDUSTRIES

WHAT COMES NEXT FOR THE MAN OF STEEL?

Against overwhelming odds, Superman has survived the destruction of his home planet, and he has saved his adopted planet and all those on it. He has found a family, fallen in love, and made a life for himself as Clark Kent. But Superman is about to face his toughest trials yet!